SLAY

SLAY

AN EROTIC TALE BY

MICHELLE MARIPOSA

Medvaja and surrounding lands

One

They galloped into the village, Princess Rhea in the lead on her bay mare. Flanking her on the left, Captain Liam, reined in his gray stallion as they slowed to avoid trampling the locals. When the villagers saw their future queen, several cheered, and Rhea permitted herself a brief smile, especially for the children.

The headman waited in the square, relief pouring into his lined face. "Your Highness." He knelt, and the other villagers did the same.

"Please rise, Harald." Rhea heard her soldiers forming up behind her, ready for orders. "Is it still near?"

Harald shook his head, rising slowly but unaided. "Long gone, Princess. It ate two sheep and terrified the shepherd, but slunk away swiftly after that."

"On foot or by wing?" Liam interrupted. His gloved hand gripped the pommel of his sword and his horse shuffled restlessly, as if eager to continue on.

"Wing, my lord," the headman bowed respectfully. "The shepherd retained enough wits to describe it. Perhaps fifteen feet long from nose to hindquarters, then that again in tail."

"Wingspan?" Rhea asked.

"The same, Highness. Thirty feet from tip to tip."

"Hm," Liam grunted. "Not a hatchling, but definitely still a juvenile. It'll need to feed again soon."

The princess lifted her gaze to the western mountains. "We need to move faster when these blasted creatures are sighted."

Harald lowered his head. "We rang the bells as soon as we knew. The shepherd sent a whistle, but it relies on someone hearing and relaying."

Rhea shook her head. "Not your fault. I'll order patrols—we've had numerous reports, but it's hard to narrow down its territory. I can't spread soldiers too thin until this damn alliance is formalized and King Thetin stops ogling our northern border."

Harald bowed. "My congratulations on your engagement, Your Highness."

A huff from Liam. "I'll have the squad scout the area where the beast attacked. Was the shepherd harmed?"

"No, my lord. I'll have him guide you."

"I'm glad to hear it," Rhea said. "We'll report back soon."

~

The ground where the sheep had been taken was churned up. The outline of panicked hoof prints beside a muddy stream revealed where the dragon had lain in wait, then plucked its meal.

Rhea lined up her boot next to a larger print—one with four talon points at the fore and a fifth to the side. Liam sidled up and murmured, "Glad that's not another man's footprint or I'd be jealous."

Rhea snorted despite the seriousness of the situation. "Like you have a problem with size."

Her captain slid his hand around her waist. "You've never complained, it's true." He pressed a kiss to her jawbone and contemplated the trees—drooping willows that would have shielded the creature from sight until too late.

Rhea sighed and leaned into him. "I take it the others are searching the area? Not a whole lot of point, is there?"

Liam chuckled and nipped her earlobe with his teeth. "There is if it gives us five minutes alone. I think we should look carefully amongst those willows—see how the dragon hid." He led her across the stream, their boots splashing in the shallows.

"Five minutes? Is that all?" she joked as they slipped between the hanging fronds.

Liam bit her neck, with just enough force to make her groan. "What I lack in time, I'll make up for in intensity, princess."

She only grinned as he unlaced her breeches with practiced hands, tugging them down and pushing her gently back against the trunk of the tree. Burying his face between her legs, he inhaled deeply. "I love your scent," he said.

She sighed, hips tilting forward as his lips placed gentle kisses at the tops of her thighs and then in between. Sighs gave way to breathy moans. She twined her fingers in his thick black hair, encouraging him. His tongue slid around her peak, teasing.

"I thought... we only... had five minutes?" she demanded in between sharp breaths.

Liam's tongue lapped straight across her center and Rhea's knees went weak. The tree kept her upright as Liam hummed appreciatively, the vibration sending her quivering into waves of pleasure. He dipped his tongue into her core, then sucked and teased hungrily until she ached to climax. Little whimpers left her lips, then a deep moan shook her as she came. A radiant smile broke across her face as her eyes closed. She felt Liam rise, pulling her breeches up and lacing them as he kissed her with tangy, delicious lips.

"Gods, you taste good," he murmured. "I could eat you for hours."

Rhea sighed, wonderfully satisfied. "The only thing that tastes better than you or me is us together," she declared, the stress of the dragon attack distant for the moment.

Liam grinned. "Perhaps tonight you could order me to your rooms and have you way with me? I dare not refuse royalty."

Rhea shoved him, rolling her eyes. "You want to play evil queen seduces noble knight? Sure. But let's report back first." They left the shelter of the willow tree and climbed the opposite bank, making their way back to the horses. The rest of the squad was returning, having found no more sign of the dragon.

"Captain?" Rhea's voice carried as she spoke more formally. "Princess?"

She smiled, far more relaxed than when they had ridden out earlier. "Thank you."

Liam bowed. "Any time, Your Highness. Any time."

Two

Reporting back to Harald took time, so the sun was setting over the mountains behind them by the time they rode through the gates of Zivalj and up to the castle. Rhea looked forward to a hot bath and an early night that included Liam's company. What she did not expect was a courtyard full of dismounting riders and the flag of Huon, borne by a standard bearer. She swore quietly. "Son of a–"

"Honored prince!" Liam called out from beside her, dismounting and approaching a handsome blonde man. The man turned, surprised, caught sight of Rhea, and broke into a smile. It took him from handsome to truly charming, and despite knowing who he was, she felt her heart skip a beat.

"Princess Rhea." The blonde prince bowed. "I had hoped to clean up before meeting you. We are somewhat travel worn after the past week."

Rhea nodded graciously, staying atop her horse for the moment. "Prince Gereon, I take it? Forgive me for not being home to greet you properly. Travel dust is secondary to hospitality." *A week's travel hasn't done him any harm*, she thought. The foreign prince made looking grubby attractive, and the easy way he wore leather armor showed he was no slouch.

She dismounted, striding forward until they were a mere yard apart, then curtseyed, unbothered by her lack of skirts. "We just rode in from a village that suffered a dragon attack earlier today," she told him. If he was surprised by her lack of courtliness, he hid it well. She wanted him to see that her duty to her people was greater than waiting around for visiting princes.

Not visiting, her mind whispered.

Gereon nodded gravely. "I'm sorry to hear it. Was anyone harmed?"

Pleased despite herself, Rhea shook her head. "A couple of sheep and one scared shepherd. We believe it's a juvenile, so it'll likely hunt again in a few days. I've ordered every town and village across the land to ring the bells if it's sighted. It's just a matter of getting there in time."

Behind, Liam cleared his throat. "Your Highness, I can show the prince and his retinue to their quarters if you like. I've no doubt your father will want to welcome them at dinner."

Rhea hid her irritation. She wasn't annoyed at her captain for speaking up, but at her evening plans being dashed. Her father would have been informed of the prince's arrival already and no doubt the servants were leaping into action to prepare the feast they had been planning for days.

"Of course. Prince Gereon, Lord Liam Cahill, captain of my guard."

Gereon's eyes assessed Liam swiftly, then gave a polite nod. "A pleasure to meet you, Lord Cahill."

As the horses were led away and the prince escorted into the castle, Rhea eyed both men briefly before turning to thank and dismiss her squad. They saluted respectfully, not looking at the newcomer, though she was sure many were tempted. No doubt they, like her, were wondering how the foreign prince would fit into their lives.

~

A feast there was, though not one as epic as the one that would mark her wedding. Rhea smiled pleasantly and engaged in conversation as her father sat between her and Prince Gereon. The semi-circular table on the dais meant that, while they were visible to the rest of the court, she was angled towards the newcomer, making it easier to gauge him.

Well-mannered without being obsequious, Gereon charmed King Denusake effortlessly. His questions showed an earnest interest in the kingdom to which he had come, and his opinions about wider politics reassured Rhea that the prince had a well-educated head on his shoulders, as well as a handsome one.

Despite this, her eyes kept sliding over to where Liam dined with a number of other knights and dames, their mail and leather exchanged for colorful dress tunics and pretty jewels. Rhea herself wore an elegant gown—silver and green brocade with a high neck, fitted sleeves and a form-hugging bodice. The long skirt swished heavily when she moved, and she enjoyed the weight on her legs.

"You do me much honor hosting me in such splendor," Gereon told her father as they finished the dessert course. "I fear my travel weariness is getting the better of me, however, and I'm surprised the princess isn't more tired from her dragon hunting today."

The king snorted even as Rhea refrained from bristling. "Rhea can outride most knights and dames, don't you worry."

Gereon saw his mistake and swiftly corrected it. "I meant no disparagement, Your Grace. I was incredibly impressed to see her highness riding in this afternoon. Not many heirs are so diligent in the stewardship of their people."

Mollified, King Denusake grunted, taking a sip of wine. "She has a strong sense of duty. She will be a great ruling queen. I'm proud of her."

"I'm right here, father," Rhea interjected tartly. "And if I'm half the monarch you are, I'll be grateful. Besides, you are going to rule for many years to come."

The king grinned affectionately and patted his daughter on the arm. "I should abdicate and enjoy my remaining years before I descend into dotage."

The princess rolled her eyes, then caught Gereon's startled expression. "He's joking. He wouldn't do that to me. Would you, father?" she intoned meaningfully.

The older man chuckled and winked at the prince. "Best acquaint yourself with our laws and customs soon, boy, lest you get put to work early!"

Rhea intervened. "Speaking of early, Prince Gereon is right—we're being rude keeping him up after he's traveled so far to be here. And I intend to be up at sunrise to train, father—you can save the carousing until after I've sorted this dragon problem."

The king conceded, and bid his daughter and the prince goodnight, kissing them on both cheeks and squeezing shoulders. "Welcome, my boy. We are glad to have you."

Three

Restlessness woke Rhea at dawn, perhaps due to the fact she hadn't had the satisfying evening she'd intended. Face down in her bed, she rocked her hips into the mattress several times before abandoning the attempt to pleasure herself. It wouldn't be as good as what she could have had if Liam had been with her.

Physical exertion was the only answer to shaking off her irritability, so she dressed and made her way to the training yard. She nodded silent greetings to the soldiers who assembled there as they prepared for their own exercises; warmups and stretches, lunges and squats, pushups and running, all before taking up weaponry to run through drills.

"May I join?"

Rhea was mildly surprised to see Prince Gereon enter the yard, dressed in a simple tunic and breeches with worn leather boots. Liam's head snapped around, but he said nothing. The rest of the men and women training ignored the interruption and continued their drills.

"Of course," she answered. It would be good to see his form if he had one. "We're working in formation, but you're welcome to join us for sparring after that."

The prince nodded his thanks, blonde hair shining with caramel-colored highlights in the morning sun. He began his own warmups while they practiced, Rhea shouting commands as they worked on a group spear defense—one designed to be used when outnumbered by enemies.

Once they'd repeated it ten times over to her satisfaction, she nodded to everyone to grab some water and take a breather.

From there, soldiers moved into pairs and the sparring began, some with swords, some spears or glaives,and some bare-fisted. She squared off against Captain Liam,
his sword against her glaive, using the long-weapon's range to neutralize the advantage his greater height and weight gave him. The bout ended without either victorious, then Liam nodded at Gereon, who had been conducting strikes and blocks with a practice sword in the air.

"Care to dance, Your Highness?"

Gereon cast his gaze over Liam's solid figure, the broad shoulders and large, scarred hands. The prince was no stripling, his muscles well-defined through fabric that clung to forming sweat, but the captain definitely had the reach.

"It would be an honor, Lord Cahill," he said, bowing, and moving into position. Rhea stepped back, interested to see how it would be handled, and if Liam would do something stupid. She needn't have worried. The match was civilized, each man testing the other's defenses, with no cheap shots or attempts to muscle through. Gereon held his own well, fast and with precise footwork that forced Liam to work hard. A round of applause pattered when both men stepped back and saluted, the other soldiers having stopped to watch.

"Well fought," Liam heaved a breath, hand on his knee. The prince, too, was breathing hard, and he bowed in acknowledgement.

"You went easy on me, I could tell."

Liam flashed a fierce smile. "I didn't think it was politic to trounce my future king on the second day he's here."

Rhea sucked in a breath. There it was. She'd refused to think about it, not wanting her dismay to be sensed. Gereon didn't deserve a disgruntled bride—marriage to him would solidify a long-tenuous alliance and provide a strong show of force against King Thetin.

"Speaking of politics," she drawled, picking up a practice sword from the nearby rack. "Would you spar with me, Your Highness? Perhaps you can teach me a few tricks from your home."

Gereon saluted, unflappably polite. "Of course, Princess."

They circled each other cautiously. It wasn't Rhea's intention to trounce the prince—after seeing him against Liam she would be the first to admit that she would have her work cut out to do that. And it would be rude, a callous display of dominance that wouldn't set a good tone for their marriage.

Gereon, too, seemed to be holding back. Of course, he didn't want to charge in and knock her on her ass—she respected his common sense for that.

"Come on, Prince." She gestured. "You can thrust your sword at me," she said, winking.

His eyebrows shot up, and a delighted smile curled his lips. It was the first time he'd shown real personality, and she was chuffed to see he had a sense of humor. He attacked, and the match began properly.

Back and forth, strike and parry—testing out each other's defenses and attracting an audience swiftly. Rhea was forced to step fast as Gereon bore down on her.

"Do you always charge in this fast?" she teased, panting.

He gave a breathless laugh. "I prefer to take things slowly, usually. But I can be flexible."

Block. Strike. Dodge. "Flexible… is… good." As if to demonstrate, she dropped into a low lunge and swiped at his leg, a killing blow with a real blade. He leaped back just in time and swung at her head.

It had been a ruse. She anticipated the move and came up, sword point resting on his throat. Gereon froze, then laughed, surrendering with good grace. "I'm glad you didn't think to strike lower, Highness. My pride couldn't have taken it."

She lowered the sword and saluted. "I've no wish to embarrass you. You could have smashed through and won, I'm sure. I appreciate you didn't."

He bowed and kissed her knuckles, looking up at her in a way that made her tingle. "I'm not a brute to charge in. I wait to be invited." A slow smile formed on his lips, then he straightened and returned his weapon to the rack.

Rhea watched him go, conscious of Liam stepping up beside her. She glanced at him, suddenly embarrassed she'd flirted so outrageously with the prince.

Her captain and lover gave her a sad smile. "He'll do well for you."

Abashed, she touched his arm. "It's my duty. We need this alliance."

Liam shrugged ironically. "Just because it's duty doesn't mean you can't enjoy it. I want to see you happy, Rhea. I knew I'd never have you forever."

Touched, she murmured, "I don't deserve you, but I'm so grateful to have you."

She moved to pack up her gear, unaware their exchange had been observed by Prince Gereon, whose unreadable polite expression had returned.

~

The rest of the morning involved dealing with matters of state alongside her father, then Rhea checked in with the steward regarding the feast that night. She spoke with several ladies of the court to discuss desired outfits for said feast, and received reports from the knights and dames in charge of patrols. She managed a nap before having to dress, still aching for Liam but also tantalized by the idea of getting to know Gereon.

Clad in a sleeveless gown of shimmering blue, struck through with threads of her signature silver, she thanked her maids as they curled her hair up into a silver tiara. Silver earbobs and a chain of spiral loops, each one attaching to the next, completed her jewelry. When she rose, the diaphanous fabric pinned to each shoulder floated like a magical cape as she moved, the skirts brushing on her thighs with each step.

Compliments abounded when she entered the main hall. Her ladies wore a similar style but in different colors, and with much more jewelry. "Like beautiful flowers," Rhea proclaimed affectionately, knowing they would make a delightful rainbow on the dance floor. She loved the enthusiasm for music and dance most of the court ladies held, and knew there would be some jostling amongst the knights and dames to secure hands that night.

"Always stunning," Liam murmured as he bowed and kissed her hand. She took his proffered arm and allowed him to escort her up to the dais where her father and Prince Gereon sat, the former smiling broadly at the beauty his daughter was, the latter looking transfixed.

"Your Grace, Your Highness." Liam bowed and retreated, leaving Rhea to curtsey and join the other royals. The symbolism of her captain's act was not lost on her, and her heart ached that it had to be so, as much as she was grateful for his graciousness.

Later in the night, after much wine and dancing, she sought a respite on a balcony overlooking Zivalj. The town lights winked as the sounds of revelry drifted up, her people having their own celebrations for her impending marriage. She sighed, wanting with all her heart to do her best for them.

"May I speak with you, Princess?" Gereon's voice was quiet as he stepped through the archway behind her.

"Of course," she replied, summoning a smile. "We are to be married soon. I imagine we will be speaking quite a bit."

He joined her at the stone railing. "About that. This alliance is important to both our peoples, for military strength as well as trade. Your father has been most welcoming but I know full well that I will be your consort, and you the ruling queen. I want to know how I can best

serve you with the skills that I have. I'm not an idle courtier; as a youngest son who was put to work as secretary for ministers, I have administrative experience, and you've seen I can fight. Let me be useful."

She blinked. "I appreciate your candor, Prince Gereon. I'm glad I don't just have to keep you like a stud horse waiting for breeding season."

He laughed, then sobered. "That is something, too, I must discuss. I know it is my duty to give you children. I also saw how Lord Cahill looks at you, and would be foolish to think a woman of your caliber has not taken lovers to date."

She stiffened, waiting for the ultimatum. "He understands my duty. You have nothing to fear from that quarter. Our heirs will be ours."

Gereon shook his head. "No, no, you misunderstand me. Just hearing soldiers and courtiers speak of you today, I understand why he feels the way he does. You are much beloved. And I do not wish to take that away from you. I am the stranger here, but it will be my home. I will contribute to the happiness of that home, to your happiness, in whatever way I can."

Nothing could be heard but the laughter and music floating up from the town below. Rhea said slowly, "I've no wish to shame you."

He shrugged. "It's no shame to share love. Have us both."

"Together, or separate?" her mouth shot off cheekily before she could stop it.

Gereon grinned, teeth glinting in the moonlight. "Both, if you wish. He's a handsome man, one I wouldn't mind at my back." He winked, then bowed. "I'll let you think on it. But I'm determined to make this alliance a success—my people deserve that."

Intrigued, Rhea had no answer until he was almost through the archway. "Prince Gereon," she called out. He halted, turning. "Come to my chamber, tonight, when the clock strikes ten." *Let him put his purse on the table,* she thought.

A devilish smile overtook his features. "It would be… my pleasure, princess."

Four

Alone in her chambers, Rhea took a deep breath when she heard the knock. "Enter," she called.

Captain Liam came in, still in his finery. His wine-red tunic clung to his broad shoulders, belted at a trim waist. She took a moment to appreciate his handsomeness, the way his large hands carefully closed the door, and the way his assured stride took him straight to her where she stood by the chaise lounge. He stopped in front of her.

"Is this the part where we spend one last night together in the throes of passion?" he asked, half joking, half hopeful.

She laughed and poured him wine, handing him the goblet. "I hope not. I wanted to discuss something with you."

His brows furrowed. "I know my place, Rhea, I'm not going to be difficult."

She shook her head, taking a seat and indicating he should do the same. "I had an interesting conversation with Prince Gereon earlier. He guessed about us, and wants to be accommodating."

Silence except for the crackle of the fire. "That's... most generous of him..." Liam said slowly. "Is it a test?"

"I don't think so. He also said he wouldn't object to you being with me... at the same time as him. Apparently he thinks you're quite handsome."

A glint appeared in Liam's eyes. "You think you can handle two men in your bed at the same time, do you?" He placed his wine down carefully.

She arched an eyebrow. "You think I can't?"

He rose, coming to stand behind her and leaning in close, hands resting on her shoulders, voice rough in her ear. "I'd like to see you try."

A knock sounded, startling all the delicious tension out of Rhea as she called out, voice tremoring slightly, "Enter."

Gereon stepped through the door, observing where she sat and Liam stood. "Should I... lock the door, Your Highness?" he asked, mouth twitching.

Rhea glanced up at Liam, whose own mouth curled into a dangerous smile. "Please do," she said, struggling to sound in control.

Gereon complied and stalked to the chaise lounge. "Lord Cahill," he nodded.

"Prince Gereon," Liam replied. "I heard you had a most intriguing proposition for our dear princess here. At least, I am intrigued. She seems to think two men is something she can handle with ease."

The prince gave a low laugh. "Well, I'd like to find out."

Rhea watched the exchange, pulse quickening. Like two wolves circling, their energies falling into sync. To be in the center, knowing that she could change the dynamic but dying to see how it would play out. Neither man was a coward, despite Liam's grace and Gereon's humility.

"Perhaps, my lord," Gereon went on, "you could show me what she likes. I am a quick study."

That excited her even more. She reached a languorous hand up to trail along Liam's forearm. His fingers tightened and he tilted her head to one side, bringing his lips down to kiss her neck.

"She loves her neck being kissed," he told Gereon, voice husky. "Being vulnerable instead of always in control. Knowing she is safe to let go." He placed a soft bite on her jaw. Rhea sighed, heat arrowing from her throat to her core. She shifted, squeezing her thighs together.

"And her waist—holding it, gripping it, running your nails across the skin there..." he went on, letting his hands slide down between the chaise and the small of her back.

"She's a sensual marvel; murmur the right words in her ear and touch her waist gently and she almost comes." Rhea arched, desperate to lose the fabric in between them.

"You are beautiful, Princess." Gereon kneeled before her, gazing at her with hunger, all his courtly politeness gone. She took his hand and placed it on her leg, right where the skirt split to mid-thigh. Following her cue, he stroked her leg, brushing the soft fabric higher each time. The sensation taunted her, and her breathing quickened.

Then Liam was guiding her mouth up to his and placing slow yet hungry kisses. His tongue stroked deep, capturing her moan. Gereon had replaced his hands with a teasing mouth, trailing small bites and soft lips up to the dampness between her legs.

"Do you like this, Your Highness?" he asked, kissing closer and closer to where she ached.

"Yes," she managed to gasp before Liam consumed her lips again. Rocking her hips upwards, she desperately needed him to know that if Gereon didn't put his tongue and mouth to work…

"Oh…" she groaned, relief rushing through her as Gereon licked straight up her center, then gently sucked on her peak. He repeated the motion, then began to swirl and taste, dipping his tongue into her then kissing as he made little noises of his own. Rhea slid sideways on the chaise, one knee bent and the other leg snaking its way around Gereon's head, urging him in.

Realizing Liam had stopped kissing her, she rolled her gaze to see him coming around the front and unlacing his breeches, shucking his jacket and tunic with alacrity. Shirt gone too, she snagged the fabric of his trousers and pulled him closer as he freed his erection.

The smell of him intoxicated her, and she took a moment to enjoy the familiar masculine scent. Guiding him closer, she took him in her mouth and moaned again, wrapped in the sensation of Gereon licking her like she was the most delicious treat he'd ever tasted, even as Liam's smooth cock slid over her tongue. Waves of pleasure spiraled up and down her body. Rhea twisted to get in a better position, growling when both men pulled away. Gereon chuckled, then drew her to her feet and kissed her as

Liam slipped her dress off her shoulders.

"You're overdressed," she told the prince between kisses. He smiled, stepping back and obligingly disrobing as Liam removed his breeches and stood behind her, hard cock nestling against her ass. He cupped her breasts, stroking her nipples with his thumbs. Gereon's own cock stood at attention as he removed the remainder of his clothing—Rhea reached towards it, tugging one of Liam's hands down to stroke between her legs.

Standing together, sighs and moans became indistinguishable as she ground herself back against Liam. Gereon kissed her, then sucked Liam's fingers as the captain lifted them from Rhea's wetness.

"I need more," she groaned. "I need you, one of you, inside me. Please."

"Your wish is always my command." Liam guided her towards the bed, gestured for Gereon to follow. "Which of us would you have first?"

She hesitated, conscious they wanted to share and pleasure her but still sensible enough of feelings to not wish to hurt the man she loved or offend the man she would marry.

"Well, I haven't had her gorgeous mouth on me, yet," said Gereon, standing at the side of the bed as he handed Rhea onto it carefully. He shot a wicked smile at Liam. "Nor yours, my lord."

Liam gave a startled laugh, then climbed onto the bed. "I think the good prince is asking us to suck his cock, my dear. I think you should start, then I'll give him something extra delicious to taste on mine." He positioned himself behind Rhea as she shifted onto all fours, taut with excitement. Liam buried his face between her legs briefly then rose to nudge her entrance with his tip. She pushed back and then rocked forwards to take Gereon in, feeling marvelously full and compressed between both men.

Groaning around the prince's cock caused him to tangle his hands in her hair, which was becoming rapidly unbound. "Gods, how do you feel so good?" Gereon muttered, fingers clutching but clearly making sure he didn't hurt her.

"Wait… till you… feel… her cunt," grunted Liam, thrusting in time. Rhea moaned again at the filthy words, so far removed from the perfectly mannered princess who danced and laughed with the young ladies of the court. She adored it when Liam spoke like this, knowing how much he loved and revered her.

"Ohhh," she moaned, the pleasure of Gereon in her mouth at the same time as Liam fucked her tipping her over the edge. She shuddered uncontrollably, Liam having to hold her hips as she sank, boneless, to the bed. He conceded her weight and laid her gently on her side as the prince knelt. She watched in thrilled fascination as he guided Liam's cock into his mouth and licked all of her creaminess off it.

"Let me repay the favor." Liam's voice had deepened, his eyes full of lust. Pulling Gereon up, the captain lay on his stomach and sucked the prince with clear skill. He caught Rhea staring and smirked, pausing to stroke Gereon's cock with his hand. "Don't act so shocked, Rhea. I was a young man in the barracks before you started looking at me as more than a friend. I know how to suck cock."

A short intake of breath preceded her hand plunging between her legs as if of its own volition. She touched herself as the two men pleasured each other, before the prince said, breathlessly, "You need to stop before I bloody well come, and our princess needs to be fucked again."

Liam grinned, giving one last lick, then moved his mouth onto one of Rhea's nipples. Lying on her back, she arched as the prince knelt between her thighs and teased her with the tip of his cock. She was so wet he slid in easily, threatening to make her climax again at the sensation wired straight into her brain. "Gods," she gasped, and he plunged into her, setting a much faster pace than Liam had before. She was glad. As wonderfully tantalizing as the slow thrusts had been before, she needed hard and fast now.

She reached out blindly, finding Liam's cock and grasped it, working up and down in a twisting motion. He groaned, kneeling upright and gripping her hair. "You're so beautiful," he rasped.

"Perfect," Gereon grunted in agreement, driving deep and making Rhea scream. It was all she could do to clutch at Liam as she came, so he took over, using his hand to bring himself to climax and spilling all over her chest. Seeing that was too much for Gereon. He pulled out and poured himself onto her stomach, almost gasping in relief.

"Mmm." Rhea closed her eyes, blissfully sated. She felt Gereon collapse beside her, resting his sweaty blonde head on her shoulder as he kissed her cheek. Liam lay on the other side, groaning softly with pleasure, hand gliding over her breasts and belly.

For a few moments, all three lay there, the scent of sex and fresh sweat imbuing them with a sense of luxurious decadence. Then Gereon gave a little laugh. "A welcome I did not expect. Better than any man could hope for."

"Hmm," Liam rumbled in his deep voice. "If you are half as dedicated to our future queen as I am, you'll always have my respect."

Rhea reached out and touched them both. "You forget I'm the one who wins here," she said lightly, hiding the powerful emotion that threatened to well up. "I've got to be the luckiest woman in the kingdom."

Liam took her hand and kissed it. "At least I know you'll enjoy your wedding night.

Five

She woke alone but satisfied, from the deep sleep of the well-rested. The pillows on either side of her still held a masculine scent, one woodsy and rich, the other slightly sweeter but no less musky.

Training was a particular delight, as the morning warmed quickly and several men, including Liam and Gereon, stripped off their shirts to spar after warmup and group drills. Yatina, a dame who held the position of lead spear in the squad, Liam's second in command, stood similarly stripped off next to Rhea, breasts bound by a leather cross-halter. Practicality more than modesty drove most of her dames. The princess considered doing the same, but watching Liam and Gereon spar shirtless took priority for the moment.

"He's handsome, Your Highness, and knows how to move," Yatina commented admiringly. "Your father did that right, when negotiating this alliance."

Rhea nodded, thinking about all the things she wanted to do with them. Letting them take the lead the night before had been good for both men—while both desired to please her, neither had been subordinate to her and she had been free to gauge their level of comfort with each other. Idly she wondered if they would pleasure each other while she watched—the quick rapport they were building as they trained was clear to see, and neither had been cock-shy. The thought made her clench and draw in a sharp breath.

"Is it too warm for you, Highness?" Yatina mostly hid her smirk, but Rhea only grinned back.

"We might need to ride out to the waterfalls for a cool off, Yatina, if this kind of weather keeps up."

Yatina sighed. "Ah, yes. Take even more clothes off and splash about. Permission to volunteer as escort, Your Highness?"

Rhea laughed. "You'll be my first pick."

She insisted to her father on no feast that night, instead dining privately with him as they discussed how to redistribute soldier patrols once the alliance with Huon had been cemented.

"There have been more dragon attacks this summer—no doubt several spring clutches that were laid in the foothills have hatched, but this last one seems to be at least a few years old." She took a bite of the salad in front of her, chewing thoughtfully.

"Perhaps driven out from the mountains by an older male? If male it is," the king replied. "Be careful hunting it, my dear— I know you are a proficient fighter, but you've not dealt with anything bigger than a cart-horse, and I would hate to see anything happen to you."

She patted his hand. "I won't endanger myself, father. We hunt in squads for a reason. Gone are the days of lone knights or dames hunting down dragons."

The king snorted. "If you believe the tapestry in the throne room, our ancestor, Queen Zané, took down a huge fire-breathing wyvern all by herself. A bit of family propaganda, if you ask me, but it did cement our bloodline as protector of our people."

Rhea shook her head. "I plan to get to this one long before it gets that big, and I have good men and women to help me."

Two of those good men were waiting in her chambers when she returned. "And who gave you permission to enter?" she asked, amused. Both Liam and Gereon watched her with hungry eyes, having risen from their quiet conversation by the window.

"Say the word and we'll leave," the prince said quietly, courtly demeanor returned.

"Don't you dare," she shot back. "I have plans for you both. Take your clothes off, if you please."

"Oh, I please," Liam smirked.

Within seconds, both men were naked and already aroused. "You're staying dressed, princess?" the captain asked, stroking her breast through the fabric of her evening dress, a sleeveless navy number less formal than the one she had worn the night before.

"I am, for now," she answered. Looking in each of their eyes, she sank slowly to her knees and leaned to breathe in their scents. Both cocks twitched as she inhaled, first Gereon, then Liam. They shuffled closer as she moved slowly between, not yet touching, just relishing the prospect.

Then she kissed Liam's shaft, sliding her tongue around its head. He moaned and Gereon moved to grip himself. "Uh uh," she said, tapping his hand away. "I'll tell you when you can touch your cock." She kissed it and swirled her tongue. A slight whimper came from the prince.

Using her hands and her mouth, Rhea switched between, sucking gently at first, then greedily. When she felt like she could take no more, she rose and pushed them back towards the bed. "Lie down," she ordered Liam, and his eyes lit with anticipation, knowing what she liked. "Stand over him," was the breathless command to Gereon as she hiked her dress and positioned herself over Liam's cock, loving the fact that her thighs were so strong from riding that she could pause and tease him. He held himself so that his tip just touched her wetness, then slid it to her peak. She moaned.

"I need to see more of you," the prince growled, grabbing her skirts and lifting the whole dress and simple shift over Rhea's head so she was naked. He was standing, as instructed, over Liam's head so that her face was the perfect height. She took him in her mouth and pushed down on Liam's cock, eyes rolling back in her head at the wonderful rightness of it all.

"Gods save me, you are just perfect, my love," Liam bucked up in time with her rhythm, looking as though it was taking everything he had not to come there and then. She couldn't see Gereon's face, the sounds the prince was making sounded like he was fighting a losing battle there too.

Rhea beat both of them to it and arched violently, crying out then clutching Gereon's legs as she collapsed forwards. Gently, lovingly, the prince lowered her onto Liam, who shifted and adjusted so that she was pressed between them as all three lay on their sides on the bed. Both men murmured endearments and praise as they kissed her hair, her shoulders, her neck, while she shuddered through the aftershocks, uttering soft cries.

Her breathing slowed, a beatific smile spreading across her face as she kissed first one, then the other, taking her time and throwing every ounce of appreciation into it. Glad of the pause but still aching with desire, Gereon ground against her ass as she kissed Liam. She rolled her hips against him, reaching back to encourage the movement. Biting her shoulder, the prince guided himself into her, both of them groaning with pleasure. Liam reached down to stroke between her legs, whispering filthy words in her ear, praising her. "Queen of my heart, better than any whore in the kingdom. Such a perfect quim, so delicious and wet, I need to taste you after he's fucked you."

Crying out again, Rhea dug her nails into Liam's arms, then gripped his cock. He jerked as if he was trying hard not to pump himself into her palm and spill everywhere. She relaxed and stroked slowly but firmly, shivering in delight as Gereon ran his nails down her back with one hand. "I want both of you," she declared hoarsely.

Liam chuckled. "You have both of us, love."

Gereon nibbled her shoulder again, then asked, voice low and thick with hunger. "Or do you mean, both inside you together, Your Highness?"

Liam's eyes blazed as he tensed, and for a moment Rhea thought he was shocked. An uncanny look spread across his face and she realized it was wicked delight. "A queen indeed," he rasped. "How would you have us?"

She rose to a sitting position and considered them both, body thrilling. "Be behind me," she breathed, looking Liam in the eyes as Gereon rolled onto his back and she mounted him, then stilled.

Liam complied, leaning so his mouth was by her ear. Voice deep, he said, "And do you want my hard cock in your cunt, with his, or in your ass, my queen of whores."

She whimpered, clenching. Gereon swore, hands kneading her thighs. "My cunt, please," she begged.

Licking his palm and rubbing his tip to make sure he was ready for her, Liam slid his cock between her ass cheeks as she rose up to meet him. Nudging gently, then firmly, feeling Gereon's cock pull out just enough to make space, Liam pushed in as the prince mimicked the move.

"Ohhhh," Rhea moaned, the fullness making her mind spasm.

"Are you alright?" Gereon asked, the concern in his voice filling Liam with renewed respect for the foreign prince.

"It's good," she responded, rocking up and down in tiny movements, working them both in as she touched between her legs. Everyone's breathing quickened as the men began to thrust gently in time, little gasps of 'yes' and 'gods, fuck, yes' escaping into the bedchamber.

The feeling of their cocks sliding together as the princess took them deeper was driving both men to the brink. Liam groaned and bit Rhea's shoulder, a matching mark to the earlier one from Gereon, whose swearing increased. She screamed in pleasure and thrust down hard, squeezing and quaking as first Liam, then Gereon, came with a shout and an almost demonic groan. Tears of ecstasy trickled down Rhea's face even as their seed tricked down her thighs.

It was several minutes of panting and more disbelieving expletives before the princess rose with a dreamy smile and disappeared into her bathing chamber for a few minutes.

Sweat cooling, Liam and Gereon straightened the bed sheets and shared a combined, satisfied smile of their own.

"She's a goddess," Gereon murmured as he settled back onto the pillows. "I must have done something incredible in a previous life to deserve to be sent here. I will worship her with every breath I have."

"We have that in common," agreed Liam, yawning, and realizing he needed to leave now if he wasn't to fall asleep on the spot. He rose.

"I didn't dismiss you." Rhea stepped out of the bathing chamber, her sultry grin warming his heart. His stupid, fatigued cock tried to twitch in answer.

"Would you have us stay, princess?" Gereon asked, failing to hide a yawn of his own.

She paused, almost back to the bed, and looked serious. "Please do, both of you."

She climbed into bed and snuggled under the blanket, leaving her lovers to copy her. Both pressed gentle kisses to her head. "Always, my love," Liam murmured as sleep overtook him. "We'll always stay."

~

"Your Highness!" The hammering on her door at dawn woke Rhea with a start. She sat bolt upright, recognizing Yatina's voice.

"Enter!" she commanded, knowing only one thing would have the dame yelling with such urgency.

Yatina strode in, then stopped abruptly, schooling her surprise into blankness. Rhea glanced to either side and realized both Liam and Gereon were in her bed, the former looking sheepish, the latter blushing with uncertainty. Rhea would have snorted with amusement, but getting dressed was of greater importance. She scooted to the foot of the bed and grabbed shirt, tunic and leggings.

"Dragon?" she asked Yatina. She sensed the men scrambling for their own clothes.

"Yes, Your Highness, a sighting near the village we visited two days ago. They rang the bells and word reached us fast. Given what you thought about its age…"

"It'll be hunting," Rhea finished. She turned to Liam. "Best spears and anyone good with a rope dart." He nodded, tucking his shirt into breeches and pulling on his boots. She turned to Gereon. "You're welcome to join, but I insist on armor, and that you hang back should it come to a fight. You're good, but you've not trained with us as a group."

"Understood, princess." He straightened his shoulders, clearly determined not to be embarrassed if she wasn't.

"Meet us in the stable yard in five minutes," she ordered. "We'll go without you if you're not there."

He bowed and left, leaving Rhea to grab her padded leathers from their stand. Yatina helped her don them, tightening straps and securing the guards.

"So… not the best morning to burst in crying dragon," the other woman observed casually.

Rhea swung around to look at her, expression searching. Seeing nothing but wry admiration on Yatina's face, she permitted herself a small smile and an apologetic shrug. "It probably would have happened eventually. It's still early days, so it didn't occur to me to check whether they were still here."

Yatina looped a steel gorget around Rhea's neck and fixed it in place. "Discretion is the better part of valor, Your Highness, and valor is part of a knight or dame's code. Can't deny I'm a little envious. If I don't get eaten by a dragon today, I might have to go find some lads to have some fun with tonight. Follow your good example."

They left the royal apartments and strode down the corridor, taking servants' stairs as a shortcut to the stables. "No one is getting eaten by a dragon today," Rhea declared. "And whatever men you choose will be delighted, I'd say, so let's hunt this wyrm down and finish it so we can both get back to doing the things we enjoy."

Despite her statement, Rhea felt the thrill of the hunt as they mounted up and checked weapons. Gereon appeared just in time, clad in light mail under a leather jerkin. Liam barked orders at his soldiers to form up, and before the sun had peeked over the horizon, they thundered down the road through Zivalj and out the northern gate.

Six

Rhea and her soldiers crept through the undergrowth, spears and rope darts held at the ready. Liam and his contingent approached from the other side of the ravine. They would wait for her signal, pinning the beast down where it consumed its stolen meal of young heifer.

As she peered over the rocky edge, her first glimpse of the creature sent her already racing heart into a gallop. Larger than any of the wyrms she'd hunted and killed in the past, she wondered whether it was just easy pickings that had drawn it out of the mountains. Older dragons rarely ventured this far, their growth supposedly slowing once they reached maturity, henceforth not needing the constant supply of fresh meat. The slow, almost delicate bites of this dragon spoke of a control that hatchlings didn't have. She had hoped to find it sated and sleeping, but at this rate, they might be waiting until nightfall, and she didn't want to risk losing the element of surprise should the beast scent them.

Sunlight winking from a shiny metal mirror told her Liam was in place on the opposite ridge. She would wait no longer.

"Attack!" she hollered, rising and swinging her rope dart into action. To her left and right, her soldiers roared and a volley of spears cascaded into the ravine. Faster than a snake, the dragon dropped its meal and whipped around, tucking wings tight as spears rained onto hard black scales. The first volley done, it did exactly as Rhea had hoped and launched itself into the air.

"Eyes and underbelly!" she commanded, spinning her rope faster and faster as the dragon rose. As it came level, she flicked her wrist and shot the dart straight out, targeting the glinting eye. The dragon jerked its head aside, and the dart skidded harmlessly along its tough neck. Cursing, Rhea hauled the rope back as the wind from the beast's wings buffeted everyone standing along the edge of the ravine.

"Spears to the wings and underbelly!" She hollered, already swinging her rope in circles for another shot before it was out of reach. "Cripple it!"

She would prefer a kill shot. Such a large monster would be devastating on the ground, even injured. The iron hard scales fended off javelins and arrows, and she wasn't letting any of her people close to that thing, even with a ten-foot pike. A glaive or normal spear might do for a smaller one, but a whipping tail could break legs as an attacker tried to get close enough to deliver a fatal blow. It was why she preferred the precision and distance of a rope dart, not to mention multiple attackers could tangle their quarry's limbs as they fought to bring down the beast together.

A defiant yell came from Yatina as she hurled her spear high, punching through the thin membrane at the edge of one wing. The loudest roar Rhea had ever heard sounded. The dragon jerked, its ascent arrested, then it lurched in the air above them. Instead of falling, it folded its wings and dove.

Straight at Rhea.

"Take cover!" she screamed, launching her rope dart as death hurtled towards her. A gout of fire tore from the dragon's mouth, incinerating rope and dart. Rhea covered her face instinctively as the heat blasted surrounding air. Pain struck her body and she couldn't breathe. *No!* she thought desperately as she braced to be burned alive.

Then her stomach lurched and cool air rushed over her just as the feeling of solid ground fell away. Her eyes flew open, blinking desperately as she realized the pain in her body came from solid bands wrapped around her torso. *Not bands… Talons.*

The wind whipped the sounds of faint screaming away. Dark scales filled her vision and great booms dominated her ears.

Wingbeats.

The dragon had her.

~

Rhea refused to pass out, but it was tempting. Clawing onto consciousness, she groaned involuntarily as they landed on a high ledge at the mouth of a great cave. The dragon placed her down surprisingly gently. She collapsed as blood flow returned sharply to various parts of her body. When her vision cleared, she fumbled for her sword, gasping at the sharp pain in her side. Were her ribs broken? On her knees, Rhea glared through tears at the monster who had brought about her doom, only to see its tail disappear into the darkness of the cave.

She kneeled alone on the ledge, high on the mountainside. Her entire kingdom lay below, stretching from the foothills to the great forest of Huon in the east. The Dagmati River flowed far to the south, through many lands all the way to the sea, though she'd never seen it. Never would now.

Breathing through the pain, Rhea managed to draw her sword. If this dragon thought to feed her to a brood of hatchlings, she wouldn't go down without a fight. For why else would it have dumped her without killing her? It obviously didn't want to eat her itself—perhaps not straight away. She shivered, the wind cutting over the clifftop.

A scraping warned her. The dragon re-emerged, moving carefully on hind legs and forepaws, wings tucked in. Rhea frowned. Her mind fought a haze of pain as she struggled to her feet, but nowhere could she see the puncture hole Yatina's spear had made.

No matter, she thought as she readied herself to die. *I'll make a few more holes of my own before it ends me.*

"Put away your pointy stick," the dragon rumbled in a deep voice. "My scales can't be pierced, even on my underbelly."

Rhea almost sat down in shock. Had the beast just *talked?* Was she hallucinating?

"Good, your mouth is open. Eat this." The dragon held a

paw to its face and blinked out a single, purple teardrop. It offered it to Rhea.

This time she did sit down, her sword clattering as it hit the ground.

"I'm going mad," she whispered. "Or I'm already dead and this is some strange afterworld that no one ever expected."

It growled. "Stop that. Eat the tear before it hardens." This close, she could smell the dragon, a great warm scent, like horse but metallic with a hint of sulfur. Not unpleasant, just unfamiliar.

Suddenly the purple teardrop was in her lap, a gelatinous blob the size of her palm. Rhea lifted it with her free hand, the other still clutching stupidly for her useless sword.

"Eat."

Raising it to her lips, Rhea bit in. Like a plum but less firm, less tart, she consumed the thing with a few, barely chewed mouthfuls and waited to see what insanity would befall her next.

Warmth radiated through her body. Her breathing eased and the pain disappeared. Strength returned and a sense of wellness pulsed throughout every limb, from her head to her feet.

"There. You are healed." The dragon sat back on its haunches and considered her. "Now we must talk."

Seven

"Our hatchlings are being murdered and it must stop."

Rhea stared up at the creature, reeling. Part of her brain was yelling at her. With difficulty, she focused on what it was trying to say. *It speaks. It's not an animal. It healed you. It hasn't killed you. You're alive.*

She croaked, "Why do other dragons not speak? You're the first one that's ever said a word."

It huffed, sending a wave of warm air rolling over her, countering the chill of the mountain breeze. It smelled like a candlewick, just extinguished. "They are hatchlings, of course they do not speak. Do human infants speak?"

She could not counter this argument, and a sick feeling in her stomach rose at the thought of killing children and babies. She steeled herself. "They raid our livestock!" she protested. "We are merely defending what it ours!" She thought for a moment. "Why do adult dragons not raid us?" The thought was terrifying. This beast—no, creature, no—what should she call it? This dragon was twice as tall as her and clearly capable of great destruction, but the old tapestries and painting in the castle showed others far larger, depicted with fiery breath and talons as long as a man. She touched her ribs gingerly, expecting pain but finding none. "How did you heal me? Why did you heal me?"

Cocking its head, the dragon gave her a long look with eyes of dark gold. Rhea shivered, and not just from the cold. Rarely had such a piercing look been sent her way.

"Come into the cave, or your frail little body will freeze." It turned and entered the dark space, leaving Rhea the choice of either freezing on the mountain ledge or following. She considered the first, affronted that the dragon thought her frail, but then decided pride would get her nowhere while she was at its mercy.

Once inside, the dragon blew little puffs of fire towards globes of crystal lodged into the ceiling. Rhea couldn't work out if the crystal spheres were natural or had been forced into the rock somehow, but when the flames dissipated, the heat and light remained, absorbed into the pale orange mineral and casting a glow. The dragon settled down, forepaws in front as it considered her, tail curled around and twitching occasionally.

"Sit, human," it said when Rhea stood awkwardly.

She frowned. "I have a name."

It snorted. "As do I, but you didn't ask for it before you started hurling spears and darts my way. If you would care to introduce yourself, I will do the same."

She crossed her arms. As princess of the kingdom, she had never needed to introduce herself and wasn't sure of the protocol. Then she realized she was worrying about protocol while in a cave with a talking dragon. She cleared her throat.

"I am Princess Rhea, heir to the kingdom of Medvaja. And you are?"

The dragon nodded in acknowledgement. "Kyan, of the Malachite Clan. My people sent me to stop the wanton murders of hatchlings. Our ranks of young warriors are dwindling and it will leave us vulnerable should other clans decide to move in on our territory."

Rhea blew out a breath, then sat down, leaning against a stalagmite. On some level, she knew how to deal with this. She had been a part of diplomatic delegations before, either with her father or on his behalf. Never mind that the other party could crush her like a beetle, it had chosen to speak instead, and now she must negotiate.

"We have never been aware that dragons were intelligent." She spread her hands in apology. "To us they are simply wild creatures that attack and take, frightening my people and even killing them. As protector of my kingdom, I have done what I believed was my duty. I am sorry this has caused harm to your kind."

Kyan huffed, whether in disapproval or disbelief, she didn't know. "Hatchlings must feed often as they grow. They do not know reason or boundaries. But I can see how killing your people would have provoked a response."

Rhea nodded cautiously. She ventured, "Why have no adult dragons such as yourself raided until now?"

"We inhabit the mountains—your lowlands are not where we wish to live. Younger dragons such as myself can hunt game capably, whereas the hatchlings need easier prey until they have developed their wits and wings. Mature dragons do not need to eat so often—they have other means of sustenance."

Rhea pondered. "You are not yet mature?" This conversation was much more candid than most diplomatic negotiations, and the frankness pleased her. She preferred not to mince words, despite her courtly upbringing.

Kyan shook its head, allowing her to admire the symmetry of the spikes and horns that flowed from its crown and down its neck. Scales she had believed to be black now hinted dark green under the crystal glow. At the ravine she hadn't noticed its color, merely its size and potential danger. Here in the cave, it bore itself with the elegance of the finest thoroughbred, but with an intelligence sharper than the sternest librarian in the royal archives.

As if it sensed her admiration, Kyan tilted its head again, raking its gaze over her armor-clad form. "I am the youngest male on our clan's council, but I am no juvenile. I will, however, grow much larger in the decades to come. And you, Princess Rhea, heir to the kingdom of Medvaja? You are an adult of your kind, and female by your scent. Clearly you are also a leader—I could tell that by the way you directed your soldiers at the ravine. It's why I brought you here—do you have the authority to treat with me?"

Rhea rankled, but suppressed her anger. "I do," she said sharply. "What is it you propose?" The healing made sense now, though she couldn't fathom the magic of how. It appeared it had healed itself as well. She now suspected the ravine had been a trap to lure her in.

Kyan lifted its—his—head and stared down imperiously. "A quota. Enough herd animals to sate our hatchlings hunger each spring until they can fend for themselves in the mountains."

"And in return?"

"You mean not simply returning with a full wing and destroying your tiny wooden homes?" Kyan said idly.

Rhea's temper rose and she shot to her feet, then she stopped. Was he... *teasing* her? She sat back down and leaned back. "Yes..." she drawled. "Since without our farmers and herders, the animals you want for your hatchlings won't flourish nearly so well. And that you healed my injuries shows good faith and a sense of honor. How did you do that, anyway?"

Kyan yawned, showing razor-sharp teeth. Rhea refused to be cowed, yawning herself as if she were bored. A rumbled chuckle emerged from the dragon's maw. "As I said, older dragons have other means of sustenance that is magical in nature. That magic is stored and regenerated when required. Tears are the simplest method."

She considered what this information could mean, whether humans would be insane enough to try to exploit that. The mountains were fraught with enough danger without seeking massive, magical winged warriors, but greed overpowered many intelligent minds, so she said, "Thank you for trusting me with this information. I see my people have been greatly mistaken about what your kind are, and I would like to rectify this. A quota of herd animals in exchange for no raids—can dragons such as you control the hatchlings so they do not attack my people or their property?"

Kyan inclined his head. "We can. For our part, we have been lax in permitting nests so far east. Breeding couples are snappish and there have been incidents, so the council decreed for everyone's safety and harmony that nests are to be far from the home caves, so couples may have peace and privacy."

"Huh." Rhea's experience with pregnancy had been nonexistent so far, but several of her dames and court ladies had given birth, and she'd witnessed the physical and emotional stress some went through, not to mention fretting husbands or partners. "How many beasts would fulfil your quota?" she asked. "And are we talking sheep, goats, cows?"

He named a figure of cows. She countered and argued that while goats were smaller, they were easier to procure and keep in the foothills. "The further your hatchlings are from settlements, the less risk to my people." She thought about how she would have to compensate those people, or whether the crown should commission flocks to be raised. They went back and forth, finally agreeing on a number.

"Some cows," Kyan insisted. "They are juicy and will sate for longer. Surely you can drive some into the hills for the spring."

She gestured, miming difficultly. "Probably, but I'll need brave men and women to do that—this detracts from my forces on the northern border. You're not the only one who has to worry about neighbors eyeing off their territory." She neglected to mention the alliance with Huon should mitigate that. She wondered what Gereon was doing now, and if the alliance was in pieces. He and Liam probably thought her dead. She needed to wrap this up and get back to them. The thought of being in their arms again warmed her—had it only been that morning she'd woken up after a night of delicious lovemaking?

Kyan inhaled sharply. "Why has your scent changed?" He extended his neck, sniffing carefully.

Rhea's eyes widened. "You can smell me?"

Still sniffling, his snout brushed her arm. She stiffened, feeling his warmth. "Of course," he rumbled. "On the ledge you reeked of fear and pain, once inside you smelt of calm defiance. Now... now you smell... on heat."

She blushed from head to toe, incredulous but fascinated. "I was thinking of my lovers." She cleared her throat. "They must think I'm dead."

"Lovers? Not one?" Kyan retreated a fraction, his gold eyes mesmerizing.

She squared her shoulders, swallowing. "My captain, Liam

Cahill—he's been a friend since childhood. And Prince Gereon, my betrothed. I am marrying him to ally Medvaja to his kingdom. But he is fast becoming more than just a political arrangement."

The dragon's eyes glittered. "So humans mate for alliances as well as breeding? And for pleasure too? Perhaps your kind are more like mine that I realized."

She breathed shallowly. "Dragons mate for pleasure?"

Kyan reached out and stroked a talon down her arm. "We do. Especially those of us who are grown but still young. Perhaps such an activity could seal our arrangement, much like the one with your prince?"

Disbelieving, Rhea rose, using the stalagmite to brace against. "Aren't there a few… physical differences that would hinder such an activity?" Was he seriously suggesting they fuck? She'd heard slurs about shepherds that spent too long out in the fields, and there was once a rumor about a dame who wanted to be mounted by a horse, but… a dragon?

Kyan's tongue flicked out and gently touched her cheek. Suddenly he seemed smaller—he was smaller! Shrinking before her eyes as the crystals in the ceiling pulsed brighter, he reared upright and spread his wings, colors sparkling in the membrane. Perhaps nine feet tall now, far larger than the tallest man but now not as… insurmountable.

Rhea swallowed. "If I mate with you, will this put the seal on our agreement?"

"It will be a bargain with a magical bond." Kyan sank to all fours again but flexed his wings. The shimmering was beautiful.

She knew about such things. Magic was little practiced in her kingdom, but she had read stories about elven mages in the south. "Then I agree." Her voice echoed in the cave.

Kyan growled and smiled, the sound deep and running straight into her core. "I'm glad." He prowled closer, meeting her eyes. "Even when afraid of me, you still showed courage." He leaned in so that his mouth was resting on her shoulder. "It is an honor to meet a warrior so fierce."

She closed her eyes, breathing him in. Tentatively raising her hands, she stroked the scales of his neck. "Hmmm," he purred. "Use your talons."

She glanced down, then removed her leather gloves. His scales were delightfully smooth under her finger tips, and when she dragged her short nails along his neck he shivered and growled again. He licked her neck, and she sucked in a sharp breath, not expecting it to feel so good.

"What… what do dragons like?" she asked, a little breathless.

He drew back and chuckled, his golden gaze capturing hers. "What do humans like? We are all different."

Emboldened, Rhea unbuckled her belt and released the clasps on her armor. "Many humans like to be naked. Not always, but your tongue on me would feel good." Stepping out of her clothes, she felt more vulnerable than she had ever felt before.

"On you?" Kyan flicked out his tongue again, this time running it across her shoulder. Rhea made a little noise.

"Yes. And here." She cupped her breasts. Kyan didn't oblige right away, building her anticipation. Then he licked slowly and deliberately across her nipples and her mouth fell open, moaning.

"Anywhere else?" he murmured. "You taste delicious."

The thought of her eating her as food melted into another thought of being eaten—her hands slid lower to guide him. "Everywhere," she begged, leaning back against the rock. His tongue roamed and teased, making her cry out
as it traced up her thighs then across her waist. He growled again.

"You smell even more delicious here." He dipped between her legs. Her body ached so much already she nearly screamed. Like a human tongue, only longer and more dexterous, he lapped her up, reaching talons around her waist to hold her steady as she rocked in ecstasy. Then he plunged his tongue into her and she did scream, the feelings so incredible it overwhelmed her. Wrapping her fingers around his horns, she fucked herself on his tongue as wetness gushed down her thighs and her knees buckled.

Kyan gently let her sink to the ground, licking his maw with evident pleasure. His eyes burned like fire, an inhuman hunger that would have frightened her had she not felt so fantastically wanton. She stared up at him, then looked lower, where what was clearly his male member had emerged from between his legs. It put her in mind of an illustration she'd seen in a book about pirates, a sea creature with eight twisting arms, and a giggling immature part of her thanked the stars Kyan's draconic cock was but one.

"May I touch?" she breathed, still languid after such wonderful release.

He growled consent, and lay on his side, exposing himself to her. She kneeled and put her hand on him, gripping, then brought her other palm down to stroke. Kyan groaned, an almost human noise, though much deeper, which excited and urged her on. Needing both hands to work him, she put her mouth on the tip. There he was barely thicker than Liam or Gereon, though the shaft widened until she could barely encircle him with both hands at the base. He was over a foot long, and while she moaned at the taste and feeling of him in her mouth, she hoped this would satisfy him. Even magically smaller, there was no way she could take him without being broken.

Kyan's tail lashed as she struggled to retain control over his twitching member. "I must have you," he growled, flipping upright and flaring his wings. He lifted her gently and held her against a nearby boulder. Covering her body with his, his cock snaked between her legs.

"You'll hurt me!" she gasped, even as the tentative nudge at her opening made her want to melt. His tail whipped from side to side, as erratic as his entry was measured.

"I won't, I promise." His cock slid achingly slow and despite her fears, Rhea pushed back. The feeling was reminiscent of having both Liam and Gereon inside her and she groaned in a way that would have made a whorehouse mistress proud. He touched her most sensitive places and sparks crossed her vision. Just when she thought she could take no more, Kyan halted and pulled back a little, then pushed in again. The rhythm he set burned away every ounce of common sense she possessed as he took her to the brink and she screamed in violent joy. Teeth grazed her shoulder and she came hard.

Boneless, she let Kyan draw her close as he settled on the ground and curled around her. She sensed a shift and realized he had returned to his original size. Her head idly resting on one forepaw, she gazed up, trying to focus through long, slow blinks. "You didn't… did you? What about your release?" she queried, yawning.

His chuckle vibrated through her as he craned his neck to gaze at her. "You are a most considerate lover, Princess Rhea. I enjoyed that most thoroughly. But I need my wits about me if I am to return you to your people, and I don't think you would appreciate me sleeping day and night."

"Oh. Thank you." She touched his chest, and yawned again. "I should dress," she declared sleepily.

"Rest a while, little human lover," Kyan purred, draping a wing over her. "I'll have you home before the sun sets."

Eight

They flew down from the mountains, the late afternoon sun streaming before them in golden shimmers on the green foothills. A sparkling stream cascading into a small waterfall caught Rhea's eye, and she tapped Kyan's shoulder hard, yelling above the wind, "Can you land there?"

He spiraled down, back-beating his wings to alight on the cliff. Rhea squeezed her knees tight and gripped his neck spikes so she wasn't dislodged. Kyan twisted his head around and asked, "What is it?"

"Could you manage down there?" She pointed to the bank next to the pool at the bottom of the waterfall. "I need water, and I should wash." She would prefer to break the news of her treaty with dragon kind without smelling of sweat and sex, just so she could better manage any misconceptions when Liam would doubtless rush up to her to make sure she was okay.

Kyan glided down to the bank, and Rhea slid off when he lowered his head to the ground. "Thank you," she said, placing a hand on his jaw. He blinked, then let his teeth peek through in a grin.

Stripping off, she hung her clothes on a tree branch and stepped ankle-deep into the icy water, bracing herself. A shocked scream escaped her when a wave drenched her body, Kyan having entered the pool and using a wing to sweep water her way.

"It's freezing!" she screeched, all dignity gone as she launched herself at him in fury. Laughing, the dragon sent another wave to impede her advance, then used his tail to lift her when she went down, spluttering.

"Wash quickly, I'll warm you up again," he promised, mischievous. Still furious, Rhea plunged under and scrubbed at herself, then stormed from the pool and made for her clothes.

"Wait," Kyan called, then a warm gust of air hit her back and her shivering lessened. He emerged and breathed on her again. "I'm sorry, that was cruel. I didn't realize the cold affects you so badly."

She turned, somewhat placated, her temper dropping as her temperature rose. "Perhaps we should arrange for a formal envoy to learn something of each other's peoples."

Kyan's form rippled and colored sparks shimmered through his wings as he magically reduced his size. "I like what I've learned so far," he murmured, nearing. Despite the warmth her nipples still stood erect. "I would like to continue that learning."

She leaned forward slightly. "Is that so?"

A flash of teeth again as he grinned and spun her using his forepaws and lowered her to all fours. Within seconds she was moaning again as his tongue slid from her peak all the way through the crease of her ass, any remaining cold she felt having fled. Rhea heard the snap of his wings flaring and relished the gentle sharpness of his talons wrapping onto her waist as the heaviness that was his cock pushed between her thighs.

Kyan didn't go so slowly this time, nor did she want him to. Thrusting back, she took him to her full extent, arching her back as blinding pleasure swept through her. "Yes, gods, yes," she cried, feeling fuller than she thought possible. Claws trailed down her naked back as he writhed inside her—Rhea came swiftly. She smiled blissfully and opened her eyes, feeling Kyan gently leave her.

Standing on the other side of the pool, their approach masked by the sound of the waterfall and her own cries, stood Liam and Gereon, mouths agape.

"Ah." She stood, a little unsteady and with a wonderful lightness in her stomach that belied the seriousness of the situation. Addressing the men, "I'm so glad you are both unharmed. Kyan of the Malachite Clan was just bringing me back. We have struck a deal whereby young dragons will no longer raid Medvajan lands." Stark naked, she summoned all her royal dignity. "I'll brief you on the details once we have returned to the Zivalj. I need to tell my father first."

Gereon turned to Liam, his blonde eyebrows raised so high they almost disappeared into his hairline. "It would appear our princess is safe, Lord Cahill."

Liam looked as though he might choke, his eyes flicking in disbelief between Rhea and Kyan, returned to full size. The dragon spoke. "An honor to make your acquaintances, Lord Cahill, and Prince Gereon, I presume. Princess Rhea and I have negotiated a treaty between our peoples. Too long have we irresponsibly let our hatchlings roam wild—our council did not realize they were such a plague on your kingdom, just as your kind did not realize that adult dragons are intelligent and can be treated with."

Liam rubbed his eyes. "Dragons are… by the stars, am I dreaming?"

Rhea cleared her throat acerbically. "You are not, captain. Please excuse me while I make myself more presentable then we may discuss. I had hoped to return by nightfall but my primary concern was assuring you both I was alive and unharmed…" she cast a glance skyward at the rapidly setting sun. "But if you are on foot, or horseback, then we are best to camp the night and set out in the daylight. Loathe as I am to worry my father longer than I must, I'll not risk either of you tramping around in the dark."

~

Kyan helpfully lit the wood gathered by Rhea and the men, and they sat around the fire eating the roast rabbit Liam had snared. She caught her captain gazing at her in perplexed wonderment before staring at Kyan, disbelieving. Gereon was trying to take it in his stride, but his baffled amusement gave him away.

Despite declaring that she would speak to the king first, Rhea gave the particulars of the quota arrangement and why, knowing she owed it to these two men who had charged off towards the mountains to rescue her. Her heart panged at their loyalty—it would have been easy to believe her dead.

"This will change everything," Liam murmured, considering the information he had just received. "Without the need to patrol the western lands for dragons, and the treaty with Huon," he shot a glance towards Gereon, "we'll be able to put a real show of force on the northern border. King Thetin won't dare threaten invasion or even raids anymore. Our people will be much safer."

Rhea eyed Gereon as well. "Does the treaty with Huon still stand?" she asked quietly. After what he'd witnessed, she knew that breaking off their engagement was a real possibility. If Liam was disgusted, she couldn't tell, but he had always loved her and understood that she always put her kingdom first. The prince, generous and adventurous a lover though he was, might not stand for the idea that his future wife willingly fucked a dragon. *And enjoyed it,* her mind whispered.

Gereon gave her a serious look, then said in the most earnest voice, "Oh, it stands. You think I'm going to walk away from being consort to the most magnificent queen in all the lands? Our children's children's children will sing songs of you."

Kyan huffed a laugh. "Your lovers are wise, princess."

Liam shot him a sharp look. "Are you including yourself in that statement, Kyan of the Malachite Clan?"

For a moment, there was only the sound of the fire crackling and the waterfall nearby, then Liam continued ironically. "Because it looks like Gereon and I need all the help we can get."

A shout of laughter burst from the prince, and Rhea shot a glare at her oldest friend. "You make me sound like some sort of sex-deranged nymph!"

Liam shrugged while Gereon howled helplessly, clutching his sides in mirth. Kyan grinned, teeth glinting in the firelight.

"What can I say, my dearest Rhea," her captain said. "If it brings peace and prosperity to the land, and allows me to keep loving you the way I do best, then long may it continue."

She gave him a long, cool look, then shook her head.

Besides," Liam winked, "it appears we three are all just as deranged as you, so it's perfect."

Rhea blushed, smiling widely, and declared, "Then here's to love and lust and duty!"